The Bracelets

Maria Edgeworth

Contents

THE BRACELETS

BY

Maria Edgeworth

THE BRACELETS.

In a beautiful and retired part of England lived Mrs. Villars, a lady whose accurate understanding, benevolent heart, and steady temper, peculiarly fitted her for the most difficult, as well as most important of all occupations--the education of youth. This task she had undertaken; and twenty young persons were put under her care, with the perfect confidence of their parents. No young people could be happier; they were good and gay, emulous, but not envious of each other; for Mrs. Villars was impartially just. Her praise they felt to be the reward of merit, and her blame they knew to be the necessary consequence of ill conduct; to the one, therefore, they patiently submitted, and in the other consciously rejoiced. They rose with fresh cheerfulness in the morning, eager to pursue their various occupations; they returned in the evening with renewed ardour to their amusements, and retired to rest satisfied with themselves and pleased with each other.

Nothing so much contributed to preserve a spirit of emulation in this little society as a small honorary distinction given annually, as the prize of successful application. The prize this year was peculiarly dear to each individual, as it was the picture of a friend whom they all dearly loved--it was the picture of Mrs. Villars in a small bracelet. It wanted neither gold, pearls, nor precious stones, to give it value.

The two foremost candidates for the prize were Cecilia and Leonora. Cecilia was the most intimate friend of Leonora, but Leonora was only the favourite companion of Cecilia.

Cecilia was of an active, ambitious, enterprising disposition; more eager in the pursuit than happy in the enjoyment of her wishes. Leonora was of a contented, unaspiring, temperate character, not easily roused to action, but indefatigable when once excited. Leonora was proud, Cecilia was vain. Her vanity made her more dependent upon the approbation of others, and therefore more anxious to please, than Leonora; but that very vanity made her, at the same time, more apt to offend. In short, Leonora was the most anxious to avoid what was wrong, Cecilia the most ambitious to do what was right. Few of their companions loved, but many were led by Cecilia, for she was often successful; many loved Leonora, but none were ever governed by her, for she was too indolent to govern.

On the first day of May, about six o'clock in the evening, a great bell rang, to summon this little society into a hall, where the prize was to be decided. A number of small tables were placed in a circle in the middle of the hall; seats for the young competitors were raised one above another, in a semicircle, some yards distant from the table; and the judges' chairs, under canopies of lilacs and luburnums, forming another semicircle, closed the amphitheatre. Every one put their writings, their drawings, their works of various kinds, upon the tables appropriated for each. How unsteady were the last steps to these tables! How each little hand trembled as it laid down its claims! Till this moment every one thought herself secure of success, but now each felt an equal certainty of being excelled; and the heart which a few minutes before exulted with hope, now palpitated with fear.

The works were examined, the preference adjudged; and the prize was declared to be the happy Cecilia's. Mrs. Villars came forward smiling, with the bracelet in her hand. Cecilia was behind her companions, on the highest row; all the others gave way, and she was on the floor in an instant. Mrs. Villars clasped the bracelet on her arm; the clasp was heard through the whole hall, and a universal smile of congratulation followed. Mrs. Villars kissed Cecilia's little hand; and "now," said she, "go and rejoice with your companions; the remainder of the day is yours."

Oh! you whose hearts are elated with success, whose bosoms beat high with joy, in the moment of triumph, command yourselves; let that triumph be moderate, that it may be lasting. Consider that, though you are good, you may be better, and though wise, you may be weak.

As soon as Mrs. Villars had given her the bracelet, all Cecilia's little companions crowded round her, and they all left the hall in an instant. She was full of spirits and vanity--she ran on, running down the flight of steps which led to the garden. In her violent haste, Cecilia threw down the little Louisa. Louisa had a china mandarin in her hand, which her mother had sent her that very morning; it was all broke to pieces by the fall.

"Oh! my mandarin!" cried Louisa, bursting into tears. The crowd behind Cecilia suddenly stopped. Louisa sat on the lowest step, fixing her eyes upon the broken pieces; then turning round, she hid her face in her hands upon the step above her. In turning, Louisa threw down the remains of the mandarin; the head, which she had placed in the socket, fell from the shoulders, and rolled bounding along the gravel-walk. Cecilia pointed to the head and to the socket, and burst out laughing; the crowd behind laughed too. At any other time they would have been more inclined to cry with Louisa; but Cecilia had just been successful, and sympathy with the victorious often makes us forget justice. Leonora, however, preserved her usual consistency. "Poor Louisa!" said she, looking first at her, and then reproachfully at Cecilia. Cecilia turned sharply round, colouring, half with shame and half with vexation. "I could not help it, Leonora," said she.

"But you could have helped laughing, Cecilia." "I didn't laugh at Louisa; and I surely may laugh, for it does nobody any harm." "I am sure, however," replied Leonora, "I should not have laughed if I had----" "No, to be sure you wouldn't, because Louisa is your favourite. I can buy her another mandarin the next time that old pedlar comes to the door, if that's all. I *can* do no more. *Can* I?" said she, turning round to her companions. "No, to be sure," said they, "that's all fair."

Cecilia looked triumphantly at Leonora. Leonora let go her hand; she ran on, and the crowd followed. When she got to the end of the garden, she turned round to see if Leonora had followed her too; but was vexed to see her still sitting on the steps with Louisa. "I'm sure I can do no more than buy her another! *Can* I?" said she, again appealing to her companions.

"No, to be sure," said they, eager to begin their plays. How many did they begin and leave off before Cecilia could be satisfied with any. Her thoughts were discomposed, and her mind was running upon something else; no wonder then that she did not play with her usual address. She grew still more impatient; she threw down the nine-pins: "Come, let us play at something else--at threading the needle," said she, holding out her hand. They all yielded to the hand which wore the bracelet. But Cecilia, dissatisfied with herself, was discontented with everybody else; her tone grew more and more peremptory,--one was too rude, another too stiff; one was too slow, another too quick; in short, everything went wrong, and everybody was tired of her humours.

The triumph of *success* is absolute, but short. Cecilia's companions at length recollected that, though she had embroidered a tulip and painted a peach better than they, yet that they could play as well, and keep their tempers better: she was thrown out. Walking towards the house in a peevish mood, she met Leonora; she passed on.

"Cecilia!" cried Leonora. "Well, what do you want with me?" "Are we friends?" "You know best." "We are; if you will let me tell Louisa that you are sorry--" Cecilia, interrupting her, "O! pray let me hear no more about Louisa!" "What! not confess that you were in the wrong! Oh, Cecilia! I had a better opinion of you." "Your opinion is of no consequence to me now; for you don't love me." "No, not when you are unjust, Cecilia." "Unjust! I am not unjust; and if I were, you are not my governess." "No, but am I not your friend?" "I don't desire to have such a friend, who would quarrel with me for happening to throw down little Louisa--how could I tell that she had a mandarin in her hand? and when it was broken, could I do more than promise her another? Was that unjust?" "But you know, Cecilia----" "*I know*," ironically, "I know, Leonora, that you love Louisa better than you do me; that's the injustice!" "If I did," replied Leonora gravely, "it would be no injustice, if she deserved it better." "How can you compare Louisa to me!" exclaimed Cecilia, indignantly.

Leonora made no answer, for she was really hurt at her friend's conduct; she walked on to join the rest of her companions. They were dancing in a round upon the grass. Leonora declined dancing, but they prevailed upon her to sing for them; her voice was not so sprightly, but it was sweeter than usual. Who sung so sweetly as Leonora? or who danced so nimbly as Louisa?

Away she was flying, all spirits and gayety, when Leonora's eyes full of tears, caught hers. Louisa silently let go her companions' hands, and quitting the dance, ran up to Leonora to inquire what was the matter with her.

"Nothing," replied she, "that need interrupt you,--Go, my dear, and dance again."

Louisa immediately ran away to her garden, and pulling off her little straw hat, she lined it with the freshest strawberry leaves, and was upon her knees before the strawberry bed when Cecilia came by. Cecilia was not disposed to be pleased with Louisa at that instant, for two reasons: because she was jealous of her, and because she had injured her. The injury, however, Louisa had already forgotten; perhaps, to tell things just as they were, she was not quite so much inclined to kiss Cecilia as she would have been before the fall of her mandarin, but this was the utmost extent of her malice, if it can be called malice.

"What are you doing there, little one?" said Cecilia in a sharp tone. "Are you eating your early strawberries here all alone?" "No," said Louisa, mysteriously; "I am not eating them." "What are you doing with them--can't you answer then? I'm not playing with you, child!" "Oh! as to that, Cecilia, you know I need not answer you unless I choose it; not but what I would, if you would only ask me civilly--and if you would not call me *child*." "Why should not I call you child?" "Because--because--I don't know;--but I wish you would stand out of my light, Cecilia, for you are trampling upon all my strawberries." "I have not touched one, you covetous little creature!" "Indeed--indeed, Cecilia, I am not covetous. I have not eaten one of them--they are all for your friend Leonora. See how unjust you are." "Unjust! that's a cant word you learned of my friend Leonora, as you call her, but she is not my friend now." "Not your friend now!" exclaimed Louisa. "Then I am sure you must have done something *very* naughty." "How!" said Cecilia, catching hold of her. "Let me go--Let me go!" cried Louisa, struggling. "I won't give you one of my strawberries, for I don't like you at all." "You don't, don't you?" said Cecilia, provoked; and catching the hat from Louisa, she flung the strawberries over the hedge. "Will nobody help me!" exclaimed Louisa, snatching her hat again, and running away with all her force.

"What have I done?" said Cecilia, recollecting herself. "Louisa! Louisa!" She called very loud, but Louisa would not turn back! she was running to her companions.

They were still dancing, hand in hand, upon the grass, whilst Leonora, sitting in the middle, sang to them.

"Stop! stop! and hear me!" cried Louisa, breaking through them; and rushing up to Leonora, she threw her hat at her feet, and panting for breath----

"It was full--almost full of my own strawberries," said she, "the first I ever got out of my own garden. They should all have been for you, Leonora, but now I have not one left. They are all gone!" said she; and she hid her face in Leonora's lap.

"Gone! gone where?" said every one at once, running up to her. "Cecilia! Cecilia!" said she, sobbing. "Cecilia!" repeated Leonora; "what of Cecilia?" "Yes, it was--it was."

"Come along with me," said Leonora, unwilling to have her friend exposed; "come, and I will get you some more strawberries." "Oh, I don't mind the strawberries, indeed; but I wanted to have had the pleasure of giving them to you."

Leonora took her up in her arms to carry her away, but it was too late.

"What, Cecilia! Cecilia, who won the prize! It could not surely be Cecilia," whispered every busy tongue.

At this instant the bell summoned them in.

"There she is!--There she is!" cried they, pointing to an arbour, where Cecilia was standing, ashamed and alone; and as they passed her, some lifted up their hands and eyes with astonishment, others whispered and huddled mysteriously together, as if to avoid her. Leonora walked on, her head a little higher than usual.

"Leonora!" said Cecilia, timorously, as she passed.

"Oh, Cecilia! who would have thought that you had a bad heart?"

Cecilia turned her head aside and burst into tears.

"Oh no, indeed, she has not a bad heart," cried Louisa, running up to her, and throwing her arms round her neck; "she's very sorry!--are not you, Cecilia? But don't cry any more, for I forgive you with all my heart; and I love you now, though I said I did not when I was in a passion."

"O, you sweet-tempered girl! how I love you," said Cecilia, kissing her.

"Well then, if you do, come along with me, and dry your eyes, for they are so red."

"Go, my dear, and I'll come presently."

"Then I will keep a place for you next to me; but you must make haste, or you will have to come in when we have all set down to supper, and then you will be so stared at! So don't stay now."

Cecilia followed Louisa with her eyes till she was out of sight. "And is Louisa," said she to herself, "the only one who would stop to pity me? Mrs. Villars told me that this day should be mine; she little thought how it would end!" Saying these words, Cecilia threw herself down upon the ground; her arm leaned upon a heap of turf which she had raised in the morning, and which in the pride and gayety of her heart, she had called her throne.

At this instant, Mrs. Villars came out to enjoy the serenity of the evening, and passing by the arbour where Cecilia lay, she started; Cecilia rose hastily.

"Who is there?" said Mrs. Villars. "It is I, madam." "And who is I?" "Cecilia." "Why, what keeps you here, my dear--where are your companions? this is, perhaps, one of the happiest days of your life."

"O no, madam!" said Cecilia, hardly able to repress her tears.

"Why, my dear, what is the matter?"

Cecilia hesitated.

"Speak, my dear. You know that when I ask you to tell me any thing as your friend, I never punish you as your governess; therefore you need not be afraid to tell me what is the matter."

"No, madam, I am not afraid, but ashamed. You asked me why I was not with my companions. Why, madam, because they have all left me, and----" "And what, my dear?" "And I see that they all dislike me. And yet I don't know why they should, for I take as much pains to please as any of them. All my masters seem satisfied with me; and you yourself, ma'am, were pleased this very morning to give me this bracelet; and I am sure you would not have given it to any one who did not deserve it." "Certainly not. You did deserve it for your application--for your successful application. The prize was for the most assiduous, not for the most amiable." "Then if it had been for the most amiable it would not have been for me?"

Mrs. Villars, smiling--"Why, what do you think yourself, Cecilia? You are better able to judge than I am. I can determine whether or no you apply to what I give you to learn; whether you attend to what I desire you to do, and avoid what I desire you not to do. I know that I like you as a pupil, but I cannot know that I should like you as a companion, unless I were your companion; therefore I must judge of what I should do by seeing what others do in the same circumstances."

"O, pray don't, ma'am; for then you would not love me neither. And yet I think you would love me; for I hope that I am as ready to oblige, and as good-natured, as----" "Yes, Cecilia, I don't doubt but that you would be very good-natured to me, but I am afraid that I should not like you unless you were good-tempered too." "But, ma'am, by good-natured I mean good-tempered--it's all the same thing." "No, indeed, I understand by them two very different things. You are good-natured, Cecilia, for you are desirous to oblige and serve your companions, to gain them praise and save them from blame, to give them pleasure, and to relieve them from pain; but Leonora is good-tempered, for she can bear with their foibles, and acknowledge her own. Without disputing about the right, she sometimes yields to those who are in the wrong. In short, her temper is perfectly good, for it can bear and forbear."

"I wish that mine could," said Cecilia, sighing.

"It may," replied Mrs. Villars; "but it is not wishes alone which can improve us in any thing. Turn the same exertion and perseverance which have won you the prize to-day to this object, and you will meet with the same success; perhaps not on the first, the second, or the third attempt, but depend upon it that you will at last; every new effort will weaken your bad habits and strengthen your good ones. But you must not expect to succeed all at once; I repeat it to you, for habit must be counteracted by habit. It would be as extravagant in us to expect that all our faults could be destroyed by one punishment, were it ever so severe, as it was in the Roman emperor we were reading of a few days ago to wish that all the heads of his enemies were upon one neck, that he might cut them off by one blow."

Here Mrs. Villars took Cecilia by the hand, and they began to walk home. Such was the nature of Cecilia's mind, that, when any object was forcibly impressed on her imagination, it caused a temporary suspension of her reasoning faculties. Hope was too strong a stimulus for her spirits; and when fear did take possession of her mind, it was attended with total debility. Her vanity was now as much mortified as in the morning it had been elated. She walked on with Mrs. Villars in silence until they came under the shade of the elm-tree walk, and then, fixing her eyes upon Mrs. Villars, she stopped short. "Do you think, madam," said she, with hesitation, "do you think, madam, that I have a bad heart?"

"A bad heart, my dear! why, what put that into your head?"

"Leonora said that I had, ma'am, and I felt ashamed when she said so."

"But, my dear, how can Leonora tell whether your heart be good or bad? However, in the first place, tell me what you mean by a bad heart."

"Indeed, I do not know what is meant by it, ma'am; but it is something which every body hates."

"And why do they hate it?"

"Because they think that it will hurt them, ma'am, I believe; and that those who have bad hearts take delight in doing mischief; and that they never do any body good but for their own ends."

"Then the best definition which you can give me of a bad heart is that it is some constant propensity to hurt others, and to do wrong for the sake of doing wrong."

"Yes, ma'am, but that is not all neither; there is still something else meant; something which I cannot express--which, indeed, I never distinctly understood; but of which, therefore, I was the more afraid."

"Well, then, to begin with what you do understand, tell me, Cecilia, do you really think it possible to be wicked merely for the love of wickedness? No human being becomes wicked all at once; a man begins by doing wrong because it is, or because he thinks it is for his interest; if he continue to do so, he must conquer his sense of shame, and lose his love of virtue. But how can you, Cecilia, who feel such a strong sense of shame, and such an eager desire to improve, imagine that you have a bad heart?"

"Indeed, madam, I never did, until every body told me so, and then I began to be frightened about it. This very evening, ma'am, when I was in a passion, I threw little Louisa's strawberries away; which, I am sure, I was very sorry for afterwards; and Leonora and every body cried out that I had a bad heart; but I am sure that I was only in a passion."

"Very likely. And when you are in a passion, as you call it, Cecilia, you see that you are tempted to do harm to others; if they do not feel angry themselves, they do not sympathize with you; they do not perceive the motive which actuates you, and then they say that you have a bad heart. I dare say, however, when your passion is over, and when you recollect yourself, you are very sorry for what you have done and said; are not you?"

"Yes, indeed, madam, very sorry."

"Then make that sorrow of use to you, Cecilia, and fix it steadily in your thoughts, as you hope to be good and happy, that, if you suffer yourself to yield to your passion upon every trifling occasion, anger and its consequences will become familiar to your mind; and in the same proportion your sense of shame will be weakened, till what you began with doing from sudden impulse you will end with doing from habit and choice; and then you would, indeed, according to our definition, have a bad heart."

"Oh, madam! I hope--I am sure I never shall."

"No, indeed, Cecilia; I do, indeed, believe that you never will; on the contrary, I think that you have a very good disposition, and, what is of infinitely more consequence to you, an active desire of improvement. Show me that you have as much perseverance as you have candour, and I shall not despair of your becoming every thing that I could wish."

Here Cecilia's countenance brightened, and she ran up the steps in almost as high spirits as she ran down them in the morning.

"Good night to you, Cecilia," said Mrs. Villars, as she was crossing the hall. "Good night to you, madam," said Cecilia; and she ran up stairs to bed.

She could not go to sleep, but she lay awake reflecting upon the events of the preceding day, and forming resolutions for the future; at the same time, considering that she had resolved, and resolved without effect, she wished to give her mind some more powerful motive; ambition she knew to be its most powerful incentive.

"Have I not," said she to herself, "already won the prize of application, and cannot the same application procure me a much higher prize? Mrs. Villars said that if the prize had been promised to the most amiable it would not have been given to me; perhaps it would not yesterday--perhaps it might not to-morrow; but that is no reason that I should despair of ever deserving it."

In consequence of this reasoning, Cecilia formed a design of proposing to her companions that they should give a prize, the first of the ensuing month (the first of June), to the most amiable. Mrs. Villars applauded the scheme, and her companions adopted it with the greatest alacrity.

"Let the prize," said they, "be a bracelet of our own hair;" and instantly their shining scissors were procured, and each contributed a lock of her hair. They formed the most beautiful gradation of colours, from the palest auburn to the brightest black. Who was to have the honour of plaiting them was now the question.

Caroline begged that she might, as she could plait very neatly, she said.

Cecilia, however, was equally sure that she could do it much better, and a dispute would inevitably have ensued, if Cecilia, recollecting herself just as her colour rose to scarlet, had not yielded--yielded with no very good grace indeed, but as well as could be expected for the first time. For it is habit which confers ease; and without ease, even in moral actions, there can be no grace.

The bracelet was plaited in the neatest manner by Caroline, finished round the edge with silver twist, and on it was worked, in the smallest silver letters, this motto, TO THE MOST AMIABLE. The moment it was completed, every body begged to try it on. It fastened with little silver clasps, and as it was made large enough for the eldest girls, it was too large for the youngest; of this they bitterly complained, and unanimously entreated that it might be cut to fit them.

"How foolish!" exclaimed Cecilia. "Don't you perceive that, if you win it, you have nothing to do but to put the clasps a little further from the edge? but if we get it, we can't make it larger."

"Very true," said they, "but you need not to have called us foolish, Cecilia!"

It was by such hasty and unguarded expressions as these that Cecilia offended; a slight difference in the manner makes a very material one in the effect. Cecilia lost more love by general petulance than she could gain by the greatest particular exertions.

How far she succeeded in curing herself of this defect, how far she became deserving of the bracelet, and to whom the bracelet was given, shall be told in the history of the first of June.

CONTINUATION OF THE BRACELETS.

The first of June was now arrived, and all the young competitors were in a state of the most anxious suspense. Leonora and Cecilia continued to be the foremost candidates; their quarrel had never been finally adjusted, and their different pretensions now retarded all thoughts of a reconciliation. Cecilia, though she was capable of acknowledging any of her faults in public before all her companions, could not humble herself in private to Leonora; Leonora was her equal, they were her inferiors; and submission is much easier to a vain mind, where it appears to be voluntary, than when it is the necessary tribute to justice or candour. So strongly did Cecilia feel this truth that she even delayed making any apology, or coming to any explanation with Leonora, until success should once more give her the palm.

If I win the bracelet to-day, said she to herself, I will solicit the return of Leonora's friendship; it will be more valuable to me than even the bracelet; and at such a time, and asked in such a manner, she surely cannot refuse it to me. Animated with this hope of a double triumph, Cecilia canvassed with the most zealous activity; by constant attention and exertion she had considerably abated the violence of her temper, and changed the course of her habits. Her powers of pleasing were now excited, instead of her abilities to excel; and, if her talents appeared less brilliant, her character was acknowledged to be more amiable; so great an influence upon our manners and conduct have the objects of our ambition. Cecilia was now, if possible, more than ever desirous of doing what was right, but she had not yet acquired sufficient fear of doing wrong. This was the fundamental error of her mind; it arose in a great measure from her early education.

Her mother died when she was very young; and though her father had supplied her place in the best and kindest manner, he had insensibly infused into his daughter's mind a portion of that enterprising, independent spirit, which he justly deemed essential to the character of her brother. This brother was some years older than Cecilia, but he had always been the favourite companion of her youth; what her father's precepts inculcated, his example enforced, and even Cecilia's virtues consequently became such as were more estimable in a man than desirable in a female.

All small objects and small errors she had been taught to disregard as trifles; and her impatient disposition was perpetually leading her into more material faults; yet her candour in confessing these, she had been suffered to believe, was sufficient reparation and atonement.

Leonora, on the contrary, who had been educated by her mother in a manner more suited to her sex, had a character and virtues more peculiar to a female; her judgment had been early cultivated, and her good sense employed in the regulation of her conduct; she had been habituated to that restraint, which, as a woman, she was to expect in life, and early accustomed to yield; compliance in her seemed natural and graceful.

Yet, notwithstanding the gentleness of her temper, she was in reality more independent than Cecilia; she had more reliance upon her own judgment, and more satisfaction in her own approbation. Though far from insensible to praise, she was not liable to be misled by the indiscriminate love of admiration; the uniform kindness of her manner, the consistency and equality of her character, had fixed the esteem and passive love of her companions.

By passive love, we mean that species of affection which makes us unwilling to offend, rather than anxious to oblige; which is more a habit than an emotion of the mind. For Cecilia, her companions felt active love, for she was active in showing her love to them.

Active love arises spontaneously in the mind, after feeling particular instances of kindness, without reflection on the past conduct or general character; it exceeds the merits of its object, and is connected with a feeling of generosity, rather than with a sense of justice.

Without determining which species of love is the more flattering to others, we can easily decide which is the most agreeable feeling to our own minds; we give our hearts more credit for being generous than for being just; and we feel more self-complacency when we give our love voluntarily, than when we yield it as a tribute which we cannot withhold. Though Cecilia's companions might not know all this in theory, they proved it in practice; for they loved her in a much higher proportion to her merits than they loved Leonora.

Each of the young judges were to signify their choice by putting a red or a white shell into a vase prepared for the purpose. Cecilia's colour was red, Leonora's white. In the morning nothing was to be seen but these shells, nothing talked of but the long-expected event of the evening. Cecilia, following Leonora's example, had made it a point of honour not to inquire of any individual her vote previous to their final determination.

They were both sitting together in Louisa's room; Louisa was recovering from the measles. Every one, during her illness, had been desirous of attending her; but Leonora and Cecilia were the only two that were permitted to see her, as they alone had had the distemper. They were both assiduous in their care of Louisa; but Leonora's want of exertion to overcome any disagreeable feelings of sensibility often deprived her of presence of mind, and prevented her being so constantly useful as Cecilia. Cecilia, on the contrary, often made too much noise and bustle with her officious assistance, and was too anxious to invent amusements and procure comforts for Louisa, without perceiving that illness takes away the power of enjoying them.

As she was sitting in the window in the morning, exerting herself to entertain Louisa, she heard the voice of an old pedlar who often used to come to the house. Down stairs she ran immediately to ask Mrs. Villars's permission to bring him into the hall.

Mrs. Villars consented, and away Cecilia ran to proclaim the news to her companions; then first returning into the hall, she found the pedlar just un-buckling his box, and taking it off his shoulders. "What would you be pleased to want, Miss?" said he. "I've all kinds of tweezer-cases, rings, and lockets of all sorts," continued he, opening all the glittering drawers successively.

"Oh!" said Cecilia, shutting the drawer of lockets which tempted her most, "these are not the things which I want; have you any china figures, any mandarins?"

"Alack-a-day, Miss, I had a great stock of that same china ware, but now I'm quite out of them kind of things; but I believe," said he, rummaging in one of the deepest drawers, "I believe I have one left, and here it is."

"Oh, that is the very thing! what's its price?"

"Only three shillings, ma'am." Cecilia paid the money, and was just going to carry off the mandarin, when the pedlar took out of his great-coat pocket a neat mahogany case; it was about a foot long, and fastened at each end by two little clasps; it had besides a small lock in the middle.

"What is that?" said Cecilia, eagerly.

"It's only a china figure, Miss, which I am going to carry to an elderly lady, who lives nigh at hand, and who is mighty fond of such things."

"Could you let me look at it?"

"And welcome, Miss," said he, and opened the case.

"O goodness! how beautiful!" exclaimed Cecilia.

It was a figure of Flora, crowned with roses, and carrying a basket of flowers in her hand. Cecilia contemplated it with delight. "How I should like to give this to Louisa," said she to herself; and at last breaking silence, "Did you promise it to the old lady?"

"O no, Miss; I didn't promise it--she never saw it; and if so be that you'd like to take it, I'd make no more words about it."

"And how much does it cost?"

"Why, Miss, as to that, I'll let you have it for half-a-guinea."

Cecilia immediately produced the box in which she kept her treasure, and emptying it upon the table, she began to count the shillings; alas! there were but six shillings. "How provoking!" said she; "then I can't have it--where's the mandarin? O I have it," said she, taking it up, and looking at it with the utmost disgust. "Is this the same that I had before?"

"Yes, Miss, the very same," replied the pedlar, who, during this time, had been examining the little box out of which Cecilia had taken her money; it was of silver.

"Why, ma'am," said he, "since you've taken such a fancy to the piece, if you've a mind to make up the remainder of the money, I will take this here little box, if you care to part with it."

Now this box was a keepsake from Leonora to Cecilia. "No," said Cecilia hastily, blushing a little, and stretching out her hand to receive it.

"Oh, Miss!" said he, returning it carelessly, "I hope there's no offence; I meant but to serve you, that's all. Such a rare piece of china-work has no cause to go a begging," added he, putting the Flora deliberately into the case; then turning the key with a jerk, he let it drop into his pocket, and lifting up his box by the leather straps, he was preparing to depart.

"Oh, stay one minute!" said Cecilia, in whose mind there had passed a very warm conflict during the pedlar's harangue. "Louisa would so like this Flora," said she, arguing with herself; "besides, it would be so generous in me to give it to her instead of that ugly mandarin; that would be doing only common justice, for I promised it to her, and she expects it. Though, when I come to look at this mandarin, it is not even so good as hers was; the gilding is all rubbed off, so that I absolutely must buy this for her. O yes, I will, and she will be so delighted! and then every body will say it is the prettiest thing they ever saw, and the broken mandarin will be forgotten forever."

Here Cecilia's hand moved, and she was just going to decide: "O! but stop," said she to herself; "consider Leonora gave me this box, and it is a keepsake; however, now we have quarreled, and I dare say that she would not mind my parting with it; I'm sure that I should not care if she was to give away my keepsake the smelling bottle, or the ring which I gave her; so what does it signify; besides, is it not my own, and have I not a right to do what I please with it?"

At this dangerous instant for Cecilia, a party of her companions opened the door; she knew that they came as purchasers, and she dreaded her Flora's becoming the prize of some higher bidder. "Here," said she, hastily putting the box into the pedlar's hand, without looking at it; "take it, and give me the Flora." Her hand trembled, though she snatched it impatiently; she ran by, without seeming to mind any of her companions--she almost wished to turn back.

Let those who are tempted to do wrong by the hopes of future gratification, or the prospect of certain concealment and impunity, remember that, unless they are totally depraved, they bear in their own hearts a monitor who will prevent their enjoying what they have ill obtained.

In vain Cecilia ran to the rest of her companions, to display her present, in hopes that the applause of others would restore her own self-complacency; in vain she saw the Flora pass in due pomp from hand to hand, each viewing with the other in extolling the beauty of the gift and the generosity of the giver. Cecilia was still displeased with herself, with them, and even with their praise; from Louisa's gratitude, however, she yet expected much pleasure, and immediately she ran up stairs to her room.

In the mean time Leonora had gone into the hall to buy a bodkin; she had just broken hers. In giving her change, the pedlar took out of his pocket, with some half-pence, the very box which Cecilia had sold him. Leonora did not in the least suspect the truth, for her mind was above suspicion; and besides, she had the utmost confidence in Cecilia. "I should like to have that box," said she, "for it is like one of which I was very fond."

The pedlar named the price, and Leonora took the box; she intended to give it to little Louisa.

On going to her room she found her asleep, and she sat down softly by her bed-side. Louisa opened her eyes.

"I hope I didn't disturb you," said Leonora.

"O no; I didn't hear you come in; but what have you got there?"

"It is only a little box; would you like to have it? I bought it on purpose for you, as I thought perhaps it would please you; because it's like that which I gave Cecilia."

"O yes! that out of which she used to give me Barbary drops. I am very much obliged to you. I always thought *that* exceedingly pretty; and this, indeed, is as like it as possible. I can't unscrew it; will you try?"

Leonora unscrewed it.

"Goodness!" exclaimed Louisa, "this must be Cecilia's box; look, don't you see a great L at the bottom of it?"

Leonora's colour changed. "Yes," she replied calmly, "I see that, but it is no proof that it is Cecilia's; you know that I bought this box just now of the pedlar."

"That may be," said Louisa; "but I remember scratching that L with my own needle, and Cecilia scolded me for it, too. Do go and ask her if she has lost her box--do," repeated Louisa, pulling her by the sleeve, as she did not seem to listen. Leonora indeed did not hear, for she was lost in thought; she was comparing circumstances, which had before escaped her attention. She recollected that Cecilia had passed her as she came into the hall, without seeming to see her, but had blushed as she passed. She remembered that the pedlar appeared unwilling to part with the box, and was going to put it again into his pocket with the half-pence; "and why should he keep it in his pocket and not show it with his other things?" Combining all these circumstances, Leonora had no longer any doubt of the truth; for though she had honourable confidence in her friends, she had too much penetration to be implicitly credulous. "Louisa," she began, but at this instant she heard a step, which, by its quickness, she knew to be Cecilia's, coming along the passage. "If you love me, Louisa," said Leonora, "say nothing about the box."

"Nay, but why not? I dare say she has lost it."

"No, my dear, I am afraid she has not." Louisa looked surprised.

"But I have reasons for desiring you not to say any thing about it."

"Well, then, I won't, indeed."

Cecilia opened the door, came forward smiling, as if secure of a good reception, and, taking the Flora out of the case, she placed it on the mantel-piece, opposite to Louisa's bed. "Dear, how beautiful," cried Louisa, starting up.

"Yes," said Cecilia, "and guess who it's for?"

"For me, perhaps!" said the ingenuous Louisa.

"Yes, take it, and keep it for my sake; you know that I broke your mandarin."

"O! but this is a great deal prettier and larger than that."

"Yes, I know it is; and I meant that it should be so. I should only have done what I was bound to do if I had only given you a mandarin."

"Well, and that would have been enough, surely; but what a beautiful crown of roses! and then that basket of flowers! they almost look as if I could smell them. Dear Cecilia! I'm very much obliged to you, but I won't take it by way of payment for the mandarin you broke; for I'm sure you could not help that; and, besides, I should have broken it myself by this time. You shall give it to me entirely, and I'll keep it as long as I live as your keepsake."

Louisa stopped short and coloured. The word keepsake recalled the box to her mind, and all the train of ideas which the Flora had banished. "But," said she, looking up wishfully in Cecilia's face, and holding the Flora doubt-fully, "did you----"

Leonora, who was just quitting the room, turned her head back, and gave Louisa a look, which silenced her.

Cecilia was so infatuated with her vanity, that she neither perceived Leonora's sign, nor Louisa's confusion, but continued showing off her present, by placing it in various situations, till at length she put it into the case, and laying it down with an affected carelessness upon the bed, "I must go now, Louisa. Good bye," said she, running up and kissing her; "but I'll come again presently;" then clapping the door after her, she went.

But as soon as the fermentation of her spirits subsided, the sense of shame, which had been scarcely felt when mixed with so many other sensations, rose uppermost in her mind. "What?" said she to herself, "is it possible that I have sold what I promised to keep for ever? and what Leonora gave me? and I have concealed it too, and have been making a parade of my generosity. O! what would Leonora, what would Louisa, what would every body think of me, if the truth were known?"

Humiliated and grieved by these reflections, Cecilia began to search in her own mind for some consoling idea. She began to compare her conduct with the conduct of others of her own age; and at length, fixing her comparison upon her brother George, as the companion of whom, from her infancy, she had been habitually the most emulous, she recollected that an almost similar circumstance had once happened to him, and that he had not only escaped disgrace, but had acquired glory by an intrepid confession of his fault. Her father's words to her brother, on that occasion, she also perfectly recollected.

"Come to me, George," he said, holding out his hand; "you are a generous, brave boy. They who dare to confess their faults will make great and good men."

These were his words; but Cecilia, in repeating them to herself, forgot to lay that emphasis on the word *men*, which would have placed it in contradistinction to the word women. She willingly believed that the observation extended equally to both sexes, and flattered herself that she should exceed her brother in merit, if she owned a fault which she thought that it would be so much more difficult to confess. "Yes, but," said she, stopping herself, "how can I confess it? This very evening, in a few hours, the prize will be decided; Leonora or I shall win it. I have now as good a chance as Leonora, perhaps a better; and must I give up all my hopes? all that I have been labouring for this month past! O, I never can;--if it were to-morrow, or yesterday, or any day but this, I would not hesitate, but now I am almost certain of the prize, and if I win it--well, why then I will--I think, I will tell all--yes, I will; I am determined," said Cecilia.

Here a bell summoned them to dinner. Leonora sat opposite to her, and she was not a little surprised to see Cecilia look so gay and unrestrained. "Surely," said she to herself, "if Cecilia had done this, that I suspect, she would not, she could not look as she does." But Leonora little knew the cause of her gayety; Cecilia was never in higher spirits, or better pleased with herself, than when she had resolved upon a sacrifice or a confession.

"Must not this evening be given to the most amiable? Whose, then, will it be?" All eyes glanced first at Cecilia and then at Leonora. Cecilia smiled; Leonora blushed. "I see that it is not yet decided," said Mrs. Villars; and immediately they ran up stairs, amidst confused whisperings.

Cecilia's voice could be distinguished far above the rest. "How can she be so happy?" said Leonora to herself. "O, Cecilia, there was a time when you could not have neglected me so!--when we were always together, the best of friends and companions, our wishes, tastes, and pleasures the same. Surely she did once love me," said Leonora; "but now she is quite changed. She has even sold my keepsake, and would rather win a bracelet of hair from girls whom she did not always think so much superior to Leonora, than have my esteem, my confidence, and my friendship, for her whole life; yes, for her whole life, for I am sure she will be an amiable woman. Oh that this bracelet had never been thought of, or that I was certain of her winning it; for I am certain that I do not wish to win it from her. I would rather, a thousand times rather, that we were as we used to be, than have all the glory in the world. And how pleasing Cecilia can be when she wishes to please! how candid she is! how much she can improve herself!--let me be just, though she has offended me--she is wonderfully improved within this last month; for one fault, and *that* against myself, should I forget all her merits?"

As Leonora said these last words, she could but just hear the voices of her companions; they had left her alone in the gallery. She knocked softly at Louisa's door----"Come in," said Louisa. "I in not asleep. Oh," said she, starting up with the Flora in her hand, the instant that the door was opened. "I'm so glad you are come, Leonora, for I did so long to hear what you were all making such a noise about--have you forgot that the bracelet----"

"O yes! is this the evening?"

"Well, here's my white shell for you. I've kept it in my pocket this fortnight; and though Cecilia did give me this Flora, I still love you a great deal better."

"I thank you, Louisa," said Leonora, gratefully. "I will take your shell, and I shall value it as long as I live. But here is a red one, and if you wish to show me that you love me, you will give this to Cecilia. I know that she is particularly anxious for your preference, and I am sure that she deserves it."

"Yes, if I could I would choose both of you; but you know I can only choose which I like the best."

"If you mean, my dear Louisa," said Leonora, "that you like me the best, I am very much obliged to you; for, indeed I wish you to love me; but it is enough for me to know it in private. I should not feel the least more pleasure at hearing it in public, or in having it made known to all my companions, especially at a time when it would give poor Cecilia a great deal of pain."

"But why should it give her pain? I don't like her for being jealous of you."

"Nay, Louisa, surely you don't think Cecilia jealous; she only tries to excel and to please. She is more anxious to succeed than I am, it is true, because she has a great deal more activity, and perhaps more ambition; and it would really mortify her to lose this prize. You know that she proposed it herself; it has been her object for this month past, and I am sure she has taken great pains to obtain it."

"But, dear Leonora, why should you lose it?"

"Indeed, my dear, it would be no loss to me; and, if it were, I would willingly suffer it for Cecilia; for, though we seem not to be such good friends as we used to be, I love her very much, and she will love me again, I'm sure she will; when she no longer fears me as a rival, she will again love me as a friend."

Here Leonora heard a number of her companions running along the gallery. They all knocked hastily at the door, calling, "Leonora! Leonora! will you never come? Cecilia has been with us this half hour."

Leonora smiled. "Well, Louisa," said she, smiling, "will you promise me?"

"O, I'm sure, by the way they speak to you, that they won't give you the prize!" said the little Louisa; and the tears started into her eyes.

"They love me though, for all that; and as for the prize, you know whom I wish to have it."

"Leonora! Leonora!" called her impatient companions; "don't you hear us? What are you about?"

"O, she never will take any trouble about any thing," said one of the party; "let's go away."

"O go! go! make haste," cried Louisa; "don't stay, they are so angry--I will, I will, indeed!"

"Remember, then, that you have promised me," said Leonora, and she left the room. During all this time Cecilia had been in the garden with her companions. The ambition which she had felt to win the first prize, the prize of superior talents and superior application, was not to be compared to the absolute anxiety which she now expressed to win this simple testimony of the love and approbation of her equals and rivals.

To employ her exuberant activity, she had been dragging branches of lilacs, and laburnums, roses, and sweet-briar, to ornament the bower in which her fate was to be decided. It was excessively hot, but her mind was engaged, and she was indefatigable. She stood still, at last, to admire her works; her companions all joined in loud applause. They were not a little prejudiced in her favour by the great eagerness which she expressed to win their prize, and by the great importance which she seemed to affix to the preference of each individual. At last, "Where is Leonora?" cried one of them, and immediately, as we have seen, they ran to call her.

Cecilia was left alone. Overcome with heat and too violent exertion, she had hardly strength to support herself; each moment appeared to her intolerably long; she was in a state of the utmost suspense, and all her courage failed her; even hope forsook her, and hope is a cordial which leaves the mind depressed and enfeebled. "The time is now come," said Cecilia; "in a few moments it will be decided. In a few moments! goodness! how much I do hazard! If I should not win the prize, how shall I confess what I have done? How shall I beg Leonora to forgive me? I, who hoped to restore my friendship to her as an honour!--they are gone to seek for her--the moment she appears I shall be forgotten--what shall--what shall I do?" said Cecilia, covering her face with her hands.

Such was her situation, when Leonora, accompanied by her companions, opened the hall-door; they most of them ran forward to Cecilia. As Leonora came into the bower, she held out her hand to Cecilia----"We are not rivals, but friends, I hope," said she. Cecilia clasped her hand, but she was in too great agitation to speak.

The table was now set in the arbour--the vase was now placed in the middle. "Well!" said Cecilia, eagerly, "who begins?" Caroline, one of her friends, came forward first, and then all the others successively. Cecilia's emotion was hardly conceivable.----"Now they are all in. Count them, Caroline!"

"One, two, three, four; the numbers are both equal." There was a dead silence.

"No, they are not," exclaimed Cecilia, pressing forward and putting a shell into the vase----"I have not given mine, and I give it to Leonora." Then snatching the bracelet, "It is yours, Leonora," said she; "take it, and give me back your friendship." The whole assembly gave a universal clap and shout of applause.

"I cannot be surprised at this from you, Cecilia," said Leonora; "and do you then still love me as you used to do?"

"O Leonora! stop! don't praise me; I don't deserve this," said she, turning to her loudly applauding companions; "you will soon despise me--O Leonora, you will never forgive me!--I have deceived you--I have sold----"

At this instant Mrs. Villars appeared--the crowd divided--she had heard all that passed from her window.

"I applaud your generosity, Cecilia," said she, "but I am to tell you that in this instance it is unsuccessful; you have it not in your power to give the prize to Leonora--it is yours--I have another vote to give you--you have forgotten Louisa."

"Louisa! but surely, ma'am, Louisa loves Leonora better than she does me!"

"She commissioned me, however," said Mrs. Villars, "to give you a red shell, and you will find it in this box."

Cecilia started, and turned as pale as death--it was the fatal box.

Mrs. Villars produced another box--she opened it--it contained the Flora--"And Louisa also desired me," said she, "to return you this Flora"--she put it into Cecilia's hand--Cecilia trembled so that she could not hold it; Leonora caught it.

"O, madam! O, Leonora!" exclaimed Cecilia; "now I have no hope left. I intended, I was just going to tell----"

"Dear Cecilia," said Leonora, "you need not tell it me; I know it already, and I forgive you with all my heart."

"Yes, I can prove to you," said Mrs. Villars, "that Leonora has forgiven you: it is she who has given you the prize; it was she who persuaded Louisa to give you her vote. I went to see her a little while ago, and perceiving, by her countenance, that something was the matter, I pressed her to tell me what it was.

"'Why, madam,' said she, 'Leonora has made me promise to give my shell to Cecilia. Now I don't love Cecilia half so well as I do Leonora; besides, I would not have Cecilia think I vote for her because she gave me a Flora.' Whilst Louisa was speaking," continued Mrs. Villars, "I saw the silver box lying on the bed; I took it up, and asked if it was not yours, and how she came by it.

"'Indeed, madam,' said Louisa, 'I could have been almost certain that it was Cecilia's; but Leonora gave it me, and she said that she bought it of the pedlar this morning. If any body else had told me so, I could not have believed them, because I remembered the box so well; but I can't help believing Leonora.'

"'But did you not ask Cecilia about it?' said I.

"'No, madam,' replied Louisa, 'for Leonora forbade me.'

"I guessed her reason. 'Well,' said I, 'give me the box, and I will carry your shell in it to Cecilia.'

"'Then, madam,' said she, 'if I must give it her, pray do take the Flora, and return it to her first, that she may not think it is for that I do it.'"

"O, generous Leonora!" exclaimed Cecilia; "but indeed, Louisa, I cannot take your shell."

"Then, dear Cecilia, accept of mine instead of it; you cannot refuse it--I only follow your example. As for the bracelet," added Leonora, taking Cecilia's hand, "I assure you I don't wish for it, and you do, and you deserve it."

"No," said Cecilia, "indeed I do not deserve it; next to you, surely, Louisa deserves it best."

"Louisa! O yes, Louisa," exclaimed every body with one voice.

"Yes," said Mrs. Villars, "and let Cecilia carry the bracelet to her; she deserves that reward. For one fault I cannot forget all your merits, Cecilia; nor, I am sure, will your companions."

"Then, surely, not your best friend," said Leonora, kissing her.

Every body present was moved--they looked up to Leonora with respectful and affectionate admiration.

"O, Leonora, how I love you! and how I wish to be like you!" exclaimed Cecilia; "to be as good, as generous!"

"Rather wish, Cecilia," interrupted Mrs. Villars, "to be as just; to be as strictly honourable, and as invariably consistent.

"Remember that many of our sex are capable of great efforts, of making what they call great sacrifices to virtue or to friendship; but few treat their friends with habitual gentleness, or uniformly conduct themselves with prudence and good sense."

The Codes Of Hammurabi And Moses
W. W. Davies

QTY

The discovery of the Hammurabi Code is one of the greatest achievements of archaeology, and is of paramount interest, not only to the student of the Bible, but also to all those interested in ancient history...

Religion   ISBN: *1-59462-338-4*   Pages:132
MSRP *$12.95*

The Theory of Moral Sentiments
Adam Smith

QTY

This work from 1749. contains original theories of conscience amd moral judgment and it is the foundation for systemof morals.

Philosophy ISBN: *1-59462-777-0*   Pages:536
MSRP *$19.95*

Jessica's First Prayer
Hesba Stretton

QTY

In a screened and secluded corner of one of the many railway-bridges which span the streets of London there could be seen a few years ago, from five o'clock every morning until half past eight, a tidily set-out coffee-stall, consisting of a trestle and board, upon which stood two large tin cans, with a small fire of charcoal burning under each so as to keep the coffee boiling during the early hours of the morning when the work-people were thronging into the city on their way to their daily toil...

Childrens   ISBN: *1-59462-373-2*   Pages:84
MSRP *$9.95*

My Life and Work
Henry Ford

QTY

Henry Ford revolutionized the world with his implementation of mass production for the Model T automobile. Gain valuable business insight into his life and work with his own auto-biography... "We have only started on our development of our country we have not as yet, with all our talk of wonderful progress, done more than scratch the surface. The progress has been wonderful enough but..."

Biographies/ ISBN: *1-59462-198-5*   Pages:300
MSRP *$21.95*

The Art of Cross-Examination
Francis Wellman

QTY

I presume it is the experience of every author, after his first book is published upon an important subject, to be almost overwhelmed with a wealth of ideas and illustrations which could readily have been included in his book, and which to his own mind, at least, seem to make a second edition inevitable. Such certainly was the case with me; and when the first edition had reached its sixth impression in five months, I rejoiced to learn that it seemed to my publishers that the book had met with a sufficiently favorable reception to justify a second and considerably enlarged edition. ..

Reference   **ISBN: *1-59462-647-2***

Pages:412
MSRP $19.95

On the Duty of Civil Disobedience
Henry David Thoreau

QTY

Thoreau wrote his famous essay, On the Duty of Civil Disobedience, as a protest against an unjust but popular war and the immoral but popular institution of slave-owning. He did more than write—he declined to pay his taxes, and was hauled off to gaol in consequence. Who can say how much this refusal of his hastened the end of the war and of slavery ?

Law   **ISBN: *1-59462-747-9***

Pages:48
MSRP $7.45

Dream Psychology Psychoanalysis for Beginners
Sigmund Freud

QTY

Sigmund Freud, born Sigismund Schlomo Freud (May 6, 1856 - September 23, 1939), was a Jewish-Austrian neurologist and psychiatrist who co-founded the psychoanalytic school of psychology. Freud is best known for his theories of the unconscious mind, especially involving the mechanism of repression; his redefinition of sexual desire as mobile and directed towards a wide variety of objects; and his therapeutic techniques, especially his understanding of transference in the therapeutic relationship and the presumed value of dreams as sources of insight into unconscious desires.

Psychology   **ISBN: *1-59462-905-6***

Pages:196
MSRP $15.45

The Miracle of Right Thought
Orison Swett Marden

QTY

Believe with all of your heart that you will do what you were made to do. When the mind has once formed the habit of holding cheerful, happy, prosperous pictures, it will not be easy to form the opposite habit. It does not matter how improbable or how far away this realization may see, or how dark the prospects may be, if we visualize them as best we can, as vividly as possible, hold tenaciously to them and vigorously struggle to attain them, they will gradually become actualized, realized in the life. But a desire, a longing without endeavor, a yearning abandoned or held indifferently will vanish without realization.

Self Help   **ISBN: *1-59462-644-8***

Pages:360
MSRP $25.45

The Rosicrucian Cosmo-Conception Mystic Christianity *by Max Heindel* ISBN: *1-59462-188-8* **$38.95**
The Rosicrucian Cosmo-conception is not dogmatic, neither does it appeal to any other authority than the reason of the student. It is: not controversial, but is: sent forth in the, hope that it may help to clear... New Age/Religion Pages 646

Abandonment To Divine Providence *by Jean-Pierre de Caussade* ISBN: *1-59462-228-0* **$25.95**
"The Rev. Jean Pierre de Caussade was one of the most remarkable spiritual writers of the Society of Jesus in France in the 18th Century. His death took place at Toulouse in 1751. His works have gone through many editions and have been republished... Inspirational/Religion Pages 400

Mental Chemistry *by Charles Haanel* ISBN: *1-59462-192-6* **$23.95**
Mental Chemistry allows the change of material conditions by combining and appropriately utilizing the power of the mind. Much like applied chemistry creates something new and unique out of careful combinations of chemicals the mastery of mental chemistry... New Age Pages 354

The Letters of Robert Browning and Elizabeth Barret Barrett 1845-1846 vol II ISBN: *1-59462-193-4* **$35.95**
by Robert Browning and Elizabeth Barrett Biographies Pages 596

Gleanings In Genesis (volume I) *by Arthur W. Pink* ISBN: *1-59462-130-6* **$27.45**
Appropriately has Genesis been termed "the seed plot of the Bible" for in it we have, in germ form, almost all of the great doctrines which are afterwards fully developed in the books of Scripture which follow... Religion/Inspirational Pages 420

The Master Key *by L. W. de Laurence* ISBN: *1-59462-001-6* **$30.95**
In no branch of human knowledge has there been a more lively increase of the spirit of research during the past few years than in the study of Psychology, Concentration and Mental Discipline. The requests for authentic lessons in Thought Control, Mental Discipline and... New Age/Business Pages 422

The Lesser Key Of Solomon Goetia *by L. W. de Laurence* ISBN: *1-59462-092-X* **$9.95**
This translation of the first book of the "Lernegton" which is now for the first time made accessible to students of Talismanic Magic was done, after careful collation and edition, from numerous Ancient Manuscripts in Hebrew, Latin, and French... New Age/Occult Pages 92

Rubaiyat Of Omar Khayyam *by Edward Fitzgerald* ISBN:*1-59462-332-5* **$13.95**
Edward Fitzgerald, whom the world has already learned, in spite of his own efforts to remain within the shadow of anonymity, to look upon as one of the rarest poets of the century, was born at Bredfield, in Suffolk, on the 31st of March, 1809. He was the third son of John Purcell... Music Pages 172

Ancient Law *by Henry Maine* ISBN: *1-59462-128-4* **$29.95**
The chief object of the following pages is to indicate some of the earliest ideas of mankind, as they are reflected in Ancient Law, and to point out the relation of those ideas to modern thought. Religiom/History Pages 452

Far-Away Stories *by William J. Locke* ISBN: *1-59462-129-2* **$19.45**
"Good wine needs no bush, but a collection of mixed vintages does. And this book is just such a collection. Some of the stories I do not want to remain buried for ever in the museum files of dead magazine-numbers an author's not unpardonable vanity...." Fiction Pages 272

Life of David Crockett *by David Crockett* ISBN: *1-59462-250-7* **$27.45**
"Colonel David Crockett was one of the most remarkable men of the times in which he lived. Born in humble life, but gifted with a strong will, an indomitable courage, and unremitting perseverance... Biographies/New Age Pages 424

Lip-Reading *by Edward Nitchie* ISBN: *1-59462-206-X* **$25.95**
Edward B. Nitchie, founder of the New York School for the Hard of Hearing, now the Nitchie School of Lip-Reading, Inc, wrote "LIP-READING Principles and Practice". The development and perfecting of this meritorious work on lip-reading was an undertaking... How-to Pages 400

A Handbook of Suggestive Therapeutics, Applied Hypnotism, Psychic Science ISBN: *1-59462-214-0* **$24.95**
by Henry Munro Health/New Age/Health/Self-help Pages 376

A Doll's House: and Two Other Plays *by Henrik Ibsen* ISBN: *1-59462-112-8* **$19.95**
Henrik Ibsen created this classic when in revolutionary 1848 Rome. Introducing some striking concepts in playwriting for the realist genre, this play has been studied the world over. Fiction/Classics/Plays 308

The Light of Asia *by sir Edwin Arnold* ISBN: *1-59462-204-3* **$13.95**
In this poetic masterpiece, Edwin Arnold describes the life and teachings of Buddha. The man who was to become known as Buddha to the world was born as Prince Gautama of India but he rejected the worldly riches and abandoned the reigns of power when... Religion/History/Biographies Pages 170

The Complete Works of Guy de Maupassant *by Guy de Maupassant* ISBN: *1-59462-157-8* **$16.95**
"For days and days, nights and nights, I had dreamed of that first kiss which was to consecrate our engagement, and I knew not on what spot I should put my lips..." Fiction/Classics Pages 240

The Art of Cross-Examination *by Francis L. Wellman* ISBN: *1-59462-309-0* **$26.95**
Written by a renowned trial lawyer, Wellman imparts his experience and uses case studies to explain how to use psychology to extract desired information through questioning. How-to/Science/Reference Pages 408

Answered or Unanswered? *by Louisa Vaughan* ISBN: *1-59462-248-5* **$10.95**
Miracles of Faith in China Religion Pages 112

The Edinburgh Lectures on Mental Science (1909) *by Thomas* ISBN: *1-59462-008-3* **$11.95**
This book contains the substance of a course of lectures recently given by the writer in the Queen Street Hail, Edinburgh. Its purpose is to indicate the Natural Principles governing the relation between Mental Action and Material Conditions... New Age/Psychology Pages 148

Ayesha *by H. Rider Haggard* ISBN: *1-59462-301-5* **$24.95**
Verily and indeed it is the unexpected that happens! Probably if there was one person upon the earth from whom the Editor of this, and of a certain previous history, did not expect to hear again... Classics Pages 380

Ayala's Angel *by Anthony Trollope* ISBN: *1-59462-352-X* **$29.95**
The two girls were both pretty, but Lucy who was twenty-one who supposed to be simple and comparatively unattractive, whereas Ayala was credited, as her Bombwhat romantic name might show, with poetic charm and a taste for romance. Ayala when her father died was nineteen... Fiction Pages 484

The American Commonwealth *by James Bryce* ISBN: *1-59462-286-8* **$34.45**
An interpretation of American democratic political theory. It examines political mechanics and society from the perspective of Scotsman James Bryce Politics Pages 572

Stories of the Pilgrims *by Margaret P. Pumphrey* ISBN: *1-59462-116-0* **$17.95**
This book explores pilgrims religious oppression in England as well as their escape to Holland and eventual crossing to America on the Mayflower, and their early days in New England... History Pages 268

QTY

The Fasting Cure *by Sinclair Upton*   ISBN: *1-59462-222-1*   **$13.95**
In the Cosmopolitan Magazine for May, 1910, and in the Contemporary Review (London) for April, 1910, I published an article dealing with my experi-
ences in fasting. I have written a great many magazine articles, but never one which attracted so much attention...   New Age/Self Help/Health Pages 164

Hebrew Astrology *by Sepharial*   ISBN: *1-59462-308-2*   **$13.45**
In these days of advanced thinking it is a matter of common observation that we have left many of the old landmarks behind and that we are now pressing
forward to greater heights and to a wider horizon than that which represented the mind-content of our progenitors...   Astrology Pages 144

Thought Vibration or The Law of Attraction in the Thought World   ISBN: *1-59462-127-6*   **$12.95**

by William Walker Atkinson   *Psychology/Religion Pages 144*

Optimism *by Helen Keller*   ISBN: *1-59462-108-X*   **$15.95**
Helen Keller was blind, deaf, and mute since 19 months old, yet famously learned how to overcome these handicaps, communicate with the world, and
spread her lectures promoting optimism. An inspiring read for everyone...   Biographies/Inspirational Pages 84

Sara Crewe *by Frances Burnett*   ISBN: *1-59462-360-0*   **$9.45**
In the first place, Miss Minchin lived in London. Her home was a large, dull, tall one, in a large, dull square, where all the houses were alike, and all the
sparrows were alike, and where all the door-knockers made the same heavy sound...   Childrens/Classic Pages 88

The Autobiography of Benjamin Franklin *by Benjamin Franklin*   ISBN: *1-59462-135-7*   **$24.95**
The Autobiography of Benjamin Franklin has probably been more extensively read than any other American historical work, and no other book of its kind
has had such ups and downs of fortune. Franklin lived for many years in England, where he was agent...   Biographies/History Pages 332

Name	
Email	
Telephone	
Address	
City, State ZIP	

☐ **Credit Card**   ☐ **Check / Money Order**

Credit Card Number	
Expiration Date	
Signature	

Please Mail to: Book Jungle
PO Box 2226
Champaign, IL 61825
or Fax to: 630-214-0564

ORDERING INFORMATION

web*: www.bookjungle.com*
email*: sales@bookjungle.com*
fax*: 630-214-0564*
mail*: Book Jungle PO Box 2226 Champaign, IL 61825*
or PayPal *to sales@bookjungle.com*

Please contact us for bulk discounts

DIRECT-ORDER TERMS

20% Discount if You Order
Two or More Books
Free Domestic Shipping!
Accepted: Master Card, Visa,
Discover, American Express